Charles George Douglas Roberts

Ave

an ode for the centenary of the birth of Percy Bysshe Shelley, August 4,

1792

Charles George Douglas Roberts

Ave

an ode for the centenary of the birth of Percy Bysshe Shelley, August 4, 1792

ISBN/EAN: 9783337387808

Printed in Europe, USA, Canada, Australia, Japan

Cover: Foto ©Andreas Hilbeck / pixelio.de

More available books at **www.hansebooks.com**

AVE:

PERCY BYSSHE SHELLEY, 1792—1892.

AVE:

AN ODE
FOR THE CENTENARY OF THE BIRTH OF
PERCY BYSSHE SHELLEY,
AUGUST 4, 1792.

BY

CHARLES G. D. ROBERTS.

———

TORONTO:
WILLIAMSON BOOK COMPANY.
1892.

PRINTED BY J. J. ANSLOW, WINDSOR, NOVA SCOTIA.

"*Thine was a lore that strives and calls*
      Outcast from home,
Burning to free the soul of man
With some new life.   How strange, a ban
Should set thy sleep beneath the walls
      Of changeless Rome!"

—BLISS CARMAN.

BY THE SAME AUTHOR.

ORION; AND OTHER POEMS. *(Out of Print.)*

IN DIVERS TONES. *(Boston: D. Lothrop Co.; and Montreal: Dawson.)*

THE CANADIANS OF OLD: A Romance, translated from the French of de Gaspé. *(New York: D. Appleton & Co.; Toronto: Hart & Riddell.)*

THE CANADIAN GUIDE BOOK. *(New York: D. Appleton & Company.)*

POEMS OF WILD LIFE: A Compilation. *(London: Walter Scott.)*

AVE:

An Ode for the Centenary of Shelley's Birth.

O tranquil meadows, grassy Tantramar,
  Wide marshes ever washed in clearest air,
Whether beneath the sole and spectral star
  The dear severity of dawn you wear,
Or whether in the joy of ample day
  And speechless ecstasy of growing June
You lie and dream the long blue hours away
    Till nightfall comes too soon,
Or whether, naked to the unstarred night,
You strike with wondering awe my inward sight,—

II.

You know how I have loved you, how my dreams
  Go forth to you with longing, though the years
That turn not back like your returning streams
  And fain would mist the memory with tears,
Though the inexorable years deny
  My feet the fellowship of your deep grass,
O'er which, as o'er another tenderer sky
    Cloud-phantoms drift and pass,—-
You know my confident love, since first, a child,
Amid your wastes of green I wandered wild.

III.

Inconstant, eager, curious, I roamed ;
  And ever your long reaches lured me on ;
And ever o'er my feet your grasses foamed,
  And in my eyes your far horizons shone.
But sometimes would you (as a stillness fell

And on my pulse you laid a soothing palm),.
Instruct my ears in your most secret spell ;
    And sometimes in the calm
Initiate my young and wondering eyes
Until my spirit grew more still and wise.

IV.

Purged with high thoughts and infinite desire
    I entered fearless the most holy place,
Received between my lips the secret fire,
    The breath of inspiration on my face.
But not for long these rare illumined hours,
    The deep surprise and rapture not for long.
Again I saw the common, kindly flowers,
      Again I heard the song
Of the glad bobolink, whose lyric throat
Pealed like a tangle of small bells afloat.

9

V.

The pounce of mottled marsh-hawk on his prey :
    The flicker of sand-pipers in from sea
In gusty flocks that puffed and fled : the play
    Of field-mice in the vetches :—these to me
Were memorable events.   But most availed
    Your strange unquiet waters to engage
My kindred heart's companionship : nor failed
      To grant this heritage,—
That in my veins for ever must abide
The urge and fluctuation of the tide.

VI.

The mystic river whence you take your name.
    River of hubbub, raucous Tantramar,
Untamable and changeable as flame,
    It called me and compelled me from afar,
Shaping my soul with its impetuous stress.

When in its gaping channel deep withdrawn
Its waves ran crying of the wilderness
    And winds and stars and dawn,
How I companioned them in speed sublime,
Led out a vagrant on the hills of Time !

VII.

And when the orange flood came roaring in
    From Fundy's tumbling troughs and tide-worn caves,
While red Minudie's flats were drowned with din
    And rough Chignecto's front oppugned the waves,
How blithely with the refluent foam I raced
    Inland along the radiant chasm, exploring
The green solemnity with boisterous haste ;
    My pulse of joy outpouring
To visit all the creeks that twist and shine
From Beauséjour to utmost Tormentine.

VIII.

And after, when the tide was full, and stilled
    A little while the seething and the hiss,
And every tributary channel filled
    To the brim with rosy streams that swelled to kiss
The grass-roots all a-wash and goose-tongue wild
    And salt-sap rosemary,—then how well content
I was to rest me like a breathless child
        With play-time rapture spent,—
To lapse and loiter till the change should come
And the great floods turn seaward, roaring home.

IX.

And now, O tranquil marshes, in your vast
    Serenity of vision and of dream,
Wherethrough by every intricate vein have passed
    With joy impetuous and pain supreme
The sharp fierce tides that chafe the shores of earth

In endless and controlless ebb and flow,
Strangely akin you seem to him whose birth
    One hundred years ago
With fiery succour to the ranks of song
Defied the ancient gates of wrath and wrong.

X.

Like yours, O marshes, his compassionate breast,
    Wherein abode all dreams of love and peace,
Was tortured with perpetual unrest.
    Now loud with flood, now languid with release,
Now poignant with the lonely ebb, the strife
    Of tides from the salt sea of human pain
That hiss along the perilous coasts of life
    Beat in his eager brain ;
But all about the tumult of his heart
Stretched the great calm of his celestial art.

Therefore with no far flight, from Tantramar
   And my still world of ecstasy, to thee,
Shelley, to thee I turn, the avatar
   Of Song, Love, Dream, Desire and Liberty;
To thee I turn with reverent hands of prayer
   And lips that fain would ease my heart of praise,
Whom chief of all whose brows prophetic wear
      The pure and sacred bays
I worship, and have worshipped since the hour
When first I felt thy bright and chainless power.

About thy sheltered cradle, in the green
   Untroubled groves of Sussex, brooded forms
That to the mother's eye remained unseen,—
   Terrors and ardours, passionate hopes, and storms
Of fierce retributive fury, such as jarred

Ancient and sceptred creeds, and cast down kings,
And oft the holy cause of Freedom marred
    With lust of meaner things,
With guiltless blood, and many a frenzied crime
Dared in the face of unforgetful Time.

XIII.

The star that burns on revolution smote
    Wild heats and change on thine ascendant sphere,
Whose influence thereafter seemed to float
    Through many a strange eclipse of wrath and fear,
Dimming awhile the radiance of thy love.
    But still supreme in thy nativity,
All dark, invidious aspects far above,
    Beamed one clear orb for thee,—
The star whose ministrations just and strong
Controlled the tireless flight of Dante's song.

15

XIV.

With how august contrition, and what tears
   Of penitential unavailing shame,
Thy venerable foster-mother hears
   The sons of song impeach her ancient name,
Because in one rash hour of anger blind
   She thrust thee forth in exile, and thy feet
Too soon to earth's wild outer ways consigned, —
     Far from her well-loved seat,
Far from her studious halls and storied towers
And weedy Isis winding through his flowers.

XV.

And thou, thenceforth the breathless child of change,
   Thine own Alastor, on an endless quest
Of unimagined loveliness, didst range,
   Urged ever by the soul's divine unrest.
Of that high quest and that unrest divine

Thy first immortal music thou didst make,
Inwrought with fairy Alp, and Reuss, and Rhine,
   And phantom seas that break
In soundless foam along the shores of Time,
Prisoned in thine imperishable rhyme.

XVI.

Thyself the lark melodious in mid-heaven ;
   Thyself the Protean shape of chainless cloud,
Pregnant with elemental fire, and driven
   Through deeps of quivering light, and darkness loud
With tempest, yet beneficent as prayer ;
   Thyself the wild west wind, relentless strewing
The withered leaves of custom on the air,
   And through the wreck pursuing
O'er lovelier Arnos, more imperial Romes,
Thy radiant visions to their viewless homes.

17

XVII.

And when thy mightiest creation thou
   Wert fain to body forth,—the dauntless form,
The all-enduring, all-forgiving brow
   Of the great Titan, flinchless in the storm
Of pangs unspeakable and nameless hates,
   Yet rent by all the wrongs and woes of men,
And triumphing in his pain, that so their fates
     Might be assuaged,—oh then
Out of that vast compassionate heart of thine
Thou wert constrained to shape the dream benign.

XVIII.

 O Baths of Caracalla, arches clad
   In such transcendant rhapsodies of green
That one might guess the sprites of spring were glad
   For your majestic ruin, yours the scene,
The illuminating air of sense and thought;

And yours the enchanted light, O skies of Rome,
Where the giant vision into form was wrought ;
    Beneath your blazing dome
The intensest song our language ever knew
Beat up exhaustless to the blinding blue !—

XIX.

The domes of Pisa and her towers superb,
    The myrtles and the ilexes that sigh
O'er San Giuliano, where no jars disturb
    The lonely aziola's evening cry,
The Serchio's sun-kissed waters,—these conspired
    With Plato's theme occult, with Dante's calm
Rapture of mystic love, and so inspired
    Thy soul's espousal psalm,
A strain of such elect and pure intent
It breathes of a diviner element.

XX.

Thou on whose lips the word of Love became
   A rapt evangel to assuage all wrong,
Not Love alone, but the austerer name
   Of Death engaged the splendours of thy song.
The luminous grief, the spacious consolation
   Of thy supreme lament, that mourned for him
Too early haled to that still habitation
     Beneath the grass-roots dim, —
Where his faint limbs and pain-o'er-wearied heart
Of all earth's loveliness became a part,

XXI.

But where, thou sayest, himself would not abide, —
   Thy solemn incommunicable joy
Announcing Adonais has not died,
   Attesting Death to free but not destroy,
All this was as thy swan-song mystical.

Even while the note serene was on thy tongue
Thin grew the veil of the Invisible,
    The white sword nearer swung, —
And in the sudden wisdom of thy rest
Thou knewest all thou hadst but dimly guessed.

XXII.

—Lament, Lerici, mourn for the world's loss!
    Mourn that pure light of song extinct at noon!
Ye waves of Spezzia that shine and toss
    Repent that sacred flame you quenched too soon!
Mourn, Mediterranean waters, mourn
    In affluent purple down your golden shore!
Such strains as his, whose voice you stilled in scorn,
        Our ears may greet no more,
Unless at last to that far sphere we climb
Where he completes the wonder of his rhyme!

XXIII.

How like a cloud she fled, thy fateful bark,
    From eyes that watched to hearts that waited, till
Up from the ocean roared the tempest dark—
    And the wild heart love waited for was still!
Hither and thither in the slow, soft tide,
    Rolled seaward, shoreward, sands and wandering shells
And shifting weeds thy fellows, thou didst hide
      Remote from all farewells,
Nor felt the sun, nor heard the fleeting rain,
Nor heeded Casa Magni's quenchless pain.

XXIV.

Thou heededst not?   Nay, for it was not thou,
    That blind, mute clay relinquished by the waves
Reluctantly at last, and slumbering now
    In one of kind earth's most compassionate graves!
Not thou, not thou,— for thou wert in the light

Of the Unspeakable, where time is not.
Thou sawest those tears ; but in thy perfect sight
      And thy eternal thought
Were they not even now all wiped away
In the reunion of the infinite day !

XXV.

There face to face thou sawest the living God
      And worshipedst, beholding Him the same
Adored on earth as Love, the same whose rod
      Thou hadst endured as Life, whose secret name
Thou now didst learn, the healing name of Death.
      In that unroutable profound of peace,
Beyond experience of pulse and breath,
      Beyond the last release
Of longing, rose to greet thee all the lords
Of Thought, with consummation in their words.

XXVI.

He of the seven cities claimed, whose eyes,
    Though blind, saw gods and heroes, and the fall
Of Ilium, and many alien skies,
    And Circe's Isle ; and he whom mortals call
The Thunderous, who sang the Titan bound
    As thou the Titan victor ; the benign
Spirit of Plato ; Job ; and Judah's crowned
        Singer and seer divine ;
Omar ; the Tuscan ; Milton vast and strong ;
And Shakspeare, captain of the host of Song.

XXVII.

Back from the underworld of whelming change
    To the wide-glittering beach thy body came ;
And thou didst contemplate with wonder strange
    And curious regard thy kindred flame,
Fed sweet with frankincense and wine and salt,

With fierce purgation search thee, soon resolving
Thee to the elements of the airy vault
    And the far spheres revolving,
The common waters, the familiar woods,
And the great hills' inviolate solitudes.

XXVIII.

Thy close companions there officiated
    With solemn mourning and with mindful tears ;—
The pained, imperious wanderer unmated
    Who voiced the wrath of those rebellious years ;
Trelawney, lion-limbed and high of heart ;
    And he, that gentlest sage and friend most true,
Whom Adonais loved.   With these bore part
    One grieving ghost, that flew
Hither and thither through the smoke unstirred
In wailing semblance of a wild white bird.

XXIX.

O heart of fire, that fire might not consume,
　　Forever glad the world because of thee ;
Because of thee forever eyes illume
　　A more enchanted earth, a lovelier sea !
O poignant voice of the desire of life,
　　Piercing our lethargy, because thy call
Aroused our spirits to a nobler strife
　　　　Where base and sordid fall,
Forever past the conflict and the pain
More clearly beams the goal we shall attain !

XXX.

And now once more, O marshes, back to you
　　From whatsoever wanderings, near or far,
To you I turn with joy forever new,
　　To you, O sovereign vasts of Tantramar !
Your tides are at the full.　Your wizard flood,

With every tribute stream and brimming creek,
Ponders, possessor of the utmost good,
    With no more left to seek ;—
' But the hour wanes and passes ; and once more
Resounds the ebb with destiny in its roar.

XXXI.

So might some lord of men, whom force and fate
    And his great heart's unvanquishable power
Have thrust with storm to his supreme estate,
    Ascend by night his solitary tower
High o'er the city's lights and cries uplift.
    Silent he ponders the scrolled heaven to read
And the keen stars' conflicting message sift,
    Till the slow signs recede,
And ominously scarlet dawns afar
The day he leads his legions forth to war.

www.ingramcontent.com/pod-product-compliance
Lightning Source LLC
Chambersburg PA
CBHW030908260626
47169CB00008B/2737